Freeze Frame

Adapted by Ellie O'Ryan

Based on the series created by Dan Povenmire & Jeff "Swampy" Marsh

Disney PRESS
New York

Printed in the United States of America
First Edition
10 9 8 7 6 5 4 3 2 1
J689-1817-1-10181

Library of Congress Catalog Card Number on file.
ISBN 978-1-4231-2741-3

For more Disney Press fun, visit www.disneybooks.com
Visit DisneyChannel.com

Part One

Chapter 1

Phineas Flynn and Ferb Fletcher grinned at each other across the dining room table as they ate dinner with their family. It had been a perfect summer day: warm sun, gentle breezes, and an exciting trip to the moon. The brothers were pretty pleased with themselves.

But across the table, their older sister, Candace Flynn, was not pleased at all. She

put down her fork and pouted. “But Mom, it’s true!” she complained. “The boys built an elevator to the moon in the backyard today!”

Mrs. Flynn shook her head. “Last time I checked, the yard was noticeably ‘moon-elevator’ free,” she said patiently.

“But—” Candace sputtered.

Phineas felt bad. He and Ferb thought Candace was a great big sister, and they didn’t mean to drive her crazy. They didn’t even mind that Candace spent most of her time trying to get them in trouble. So Phineas decided to speak up in her defense.

“It’s true,” he said, nodding his head. “We *were* up there. Ferb did the whole ‘one giant step’ thing. Check out this moon stuff we brought back.” He held out a handful of moon rocks, while Ferb waved an American flag—the one that Neil Armstrong had planted forty years earlier!

Candace crossed her arms and smirked.

But their mother just smiled at Phineas and Ferb.

Their dad smiled at them, too. "Oh, you boys are so adorable," Mr. Fletcher said proudly.

"Ugh! You don't believe it?" Candace shrieked. "I'm *so* over this!"

"Oh, Candace," her mom said with a sigh. "Revel in your brothers' imaginations. It makes life so much more

fun!" She stood up and started to clear the table.

Phineas stretched and yawned. "Pushing the boundaries of time and space sure makes a guy tired," he remarked.

"See?" Mrs. Flynn asked, looking at Candace. "How fun is that?"

But Candace just shook her head. She didn't think there was anything fun about living with Phineas and Ferb. In fact, ever since they had all moved in together and Ferb had officially become her stepbrother, Candace had been constantly annoyed by the pair. They did one crazy thing after another—and they *never* got in trouble for any of it!

But Phineas and Ferb had been thrilled when Phineas's mom married Ferb's dad. They felt more like real brothers than stepbrothers—and, even better, they were best friends, too!

Phineas and Ferb got up from the table and walked over to the staircase. After their exciting adventures that day, they were ready for bed.

"'Night, boys," Mr. Fletcher called to them.

"'Night, mopey," Mrs. Flynn teased Candace.

Candace slumped off toward the stairs without even responding to her mom. No matter what shenanigans Phineas and Ferb pulled, no one ever believed Candace. Her parents always thought *she* was the crazy one!

"'See? How fun is that?'" she said grumpily, mimicking her mother. "If only they'd believe me!" But Candace knew that without cold, hard, undeniable proof, Phineas and Ferb would continue to get away with their usual stunts.

In the kitchen, Mr. Fletcher started to open the day's mail, where he found an unpleasant surprise. A frown crossed his face.

"Look at this," he complained. "I've got a traffic ticket from that camera that they

installed across the street. Oh, that blasted device picks up everything on the block twenty-four hours a day!"

Candace paused as she was about to climb the stairs. She knew she shouldn't eavesdrop—but this sounded too important to miss.

"Doesn't it run out of tape?" Mrs. Flynn asked.

"Oh, no—it's on a compressed CD thingamabob. It can store months of digital video," he replied.

"You *know* we drive on the right," Mrs. Flynn reminded her husband for the hundredth time. She thought maybe that was why he had gotten a ticket.

Mr. Fletcher, however, was used to driving

on the left side of the road, the way everyone did in the United Kingdom. "Yes, yes, so you keep telling me," he replied.

But Candace wasn't listening to her parents anymore. She ran over and peered out the window in the front door. Right across the street, mounted on a streetlamp, a video camera glinted in the moonlight.

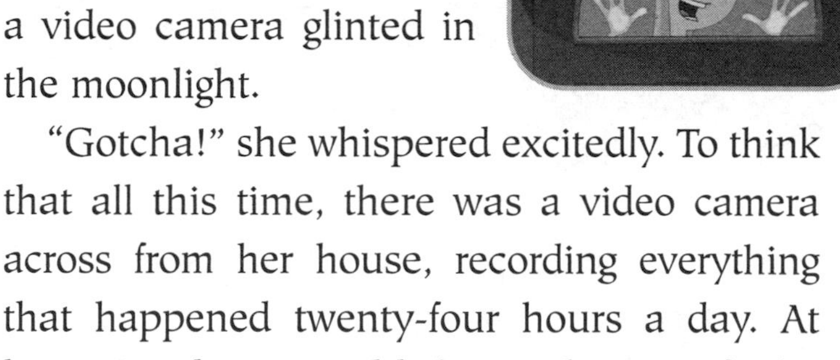

"Gotcha!" she whispered excitedly. To think that all this time, there was a video camera across from her house, recording everything that happened twenty-four hours a day. At last, Candace would have the proof she needed to expose all of Phineas and Ferb's crazy stunts!

And she couldn't wait to show the world!

Later that night, while everyone was asleep, Perry, the family's pet platypus who was in

a deep slumber on Ferb's bed, was rudely awakened. His wristwatch's silent alarm was vibrating. For Perry was no ordinary platypus.

He was the top secret operative Agent P, who dedicated his life to fighting crime. His greatest enemy was Dr. Doofenshmirtz, an evil mastermind who had a seemingly endless supply of wicked plots that he couldn't wait to unleash on the tri-state area.

Perry slapped a dark fedora on his head, instantly transforming himself into Agent P. He then dove into what looked like an ordinary top hat on Ferb's bedside table. But it was actually a portal that transported Agent P directly to his secret lair, where he popped out of a second top hat.

Just then, an image of Major Monogram, Agent P's superior officer, appeared on a giant TV screen. He clapped appreciatively as Agent P took a bow.

"Excellent trick, Agent P," Major Monogram said merrily. Then he got down to business. "Sorry to disturb you at this late hour, but we are about to give you the most important mission of your career. Our computer indicates that a

city security camera located near your civilian hideout has recorded your comings and goings as a secret agent."

Major Monogram's face disappeared as the screen showed an image of the camera capturing one of Agent P's remarkable secret agent moves: sneaking off to his agency's headquarters through a hollow tree.

"It's crucial to the agency's security that you get those recordings and bring them back to headquarters for special disposal," Major Monogram continued.

The platypus nodded and saluted. This was an extremely important mission, and Agent P was on the case!

Chapter 2

Agent P hurried home as fast as he could. He needed to get the disk that contained the recordings and deliver it to the agency's headquarters before there was any chance of his identity being discovered.

But the platypus wasn't the only one who had big plans for those recordings. With a wide smile on her face, Candace skipped down the street, carrying a giant ladder.

"La-da-da-da-da," she hummed, trying to sound casual as she climbed up the ladder to reach the camera. She slyly opened the camera, removed the CD, and slipped it into her pocket. At last she had the proof she desperately needed to bust her little brothers!

From the bushes beneath the streetlight, Agent P frowned as he watched Candace take the CD. But he wouldn't let this little glitch throw off his plans. He would figure something out!

Candace climbed down the

ladder and raced back into the house, running to her bedroom. She couldn't wait to watch the CD and all its secret footage! She popped it into her laptop and curled up on a seat by the window, eager to see Phineas and Ferb at their best . . . or, even better, at their worst!

She didn't have long to wait. An image of Phineas and Ferb's elevator to the moon appeared on the screen immediately.

"There it is!" Candace gasped. "The elevator to the moon!"

And that wasn't the only adventure caught on tape. One by one, crazy images filled the screen. "And the time they built the roller

coaster! And the beach! *And* the roller rink!" Candace exclaimed. The footage was even better than she had imagined!

Candace buried her face in a heart-covered pillow to muffle her squeals of glee. Outside, Agent P peeked in the window just in time to see an image of himself piloting a flying car. He narrowed his eyes. It was just as Major Monogram had suspected: the CD was filled with evidence that would reveal Agent P's secret identity!

The platypus knew that all he had to do was wait until Candace's back was turned, then take the CD out of her laptop and dash back to his agency's headquarters. It would have been an easy task—if Candace wasn't so excited. Instead of calmly moving away from the laptop, she was bouncing back and forth happily. Agent P had to constantly turn back into regular old Perry just to keep his cover from being blown.

"Can it be? Actual proof of *everything* they've done over the summer?" Candace asked aloud.

Just then, the door to Candace's bedroom flew open. Phineas and Ferb burst into the room—without knocking, as usual.

"Candace, you okay?" Phineas asked. Her loud shrieks had woken them up. Then he glanced at the laptop. "What are you watching?"

Candace's eyes gleamed as she studied the computer screen. "Oh, just a little summer miniseries . . . called *evidence*!" she cried, showing the laptop to her brothers.

"Oh, cool, our moon elevator!" Phineas

exclaimed. "Mom would love this! I wonder if she's still up. Let's show her!"

"Yes," Candace replied happily, agreeing with Phineas for probably the first time in her life. "Let's show Mom!"

As Phineas and Ferb hurried off to their parents' bedroom, Candace started to pace back and forth. "Oh, Perry, Perry, Perry," she said. "I will remember this night always! Just think, on this very computer are the deliciously incriminating images from that CD I borrowed that will finally bust my brothers!"

While Candace paced, Agent P plotted. Surely he could grab the CD before Candace turned back around—but she was moving too quickly for even the great Agent P.

As Candace started to laugh uncontrollably, her mother burst into the room wearing a frilly nightgown and hot pink curlers in her hair.

She did not look happy to be awake. Phineas and Ferb followed behind her.

"All right, Candace," Mrs. Flynn said with a yawn. "What's going on?"

Candace beamed. At last, her big moment had arrived! She took a deep breath. "Mom, I *finally* got the evidence that will prove—"

But her mother didn't give her a chance to finish. "Oh! Not this again," Mrs. Flynn interrupted. "Show me in the morning."

"How's seven o'clock sound?" Phineas asked her.

"And you two—out of here," their mom

added as she headed back to bed.

"We're going to pencil her in for seven-thirty," Phineas announced.

"Nine!" Mrs. Flynn called from her bedroom.

"Make that nine o'clock," Phineas replied. He wished he didn't have to wait so long to show his mom all of the summer's amazing adventures. But he figured it was better late than never!

Chapter 3

Across town, at the headquarters of Doofenshmirtz Evil, Incorporated, Agent P banged on the door. The situation with the CD was getting out of hand—which meant it was time to turn to desperate measures.

A sleepy Dr. Doofenshmirtz opened the door. "What i*th* it?" he lisped as he rubbed his eyes. "Oh, Perry the Platypu*th*! Hold on one *th*econd."

Dr. Doofenshmirtz reached into his mouth and removed a plastic bite guard from his teeth. "What? It's the pressures of an evil life. I need a grind guard," he replied in response to Agent P's stare. Then Dr. Doofenshmirtz frowned. "Wait a minute. Why are you here? You're not due to shatter my plans until tomorrow."

But Agent P had no time to waste. He raced past Dr. Doofenshmirtz into the building.

"Oh, come on in," Dr. Doofenshmirtz said with a sigh. He followed Agent P down the hall to his bedroom. Agent P flung open a door to a tall closet. Inside was a giant robot in the form of a man!

The robot's teeth glowed green as it grinned. "Hi, I'm Norm!" it announced in a friendly, robotic voice.

"That's *it*?" asked Dr. Doofenshmirtz. "You just want to borrow Norm, my giant robot man? Fine. Knock yourself out. I'm going back to bed."

As Dr. Doofenshmirtz stumbled back to his room, Agent P climbed up the robot to the control station located in its head.

"Just so you know, he's a little low on oil," Dr. Doofenshmirtz called out. "Oh, and Perry the Platypus—" Dr. Doofenshmirtz paused as he replaced his bite guard. "I don't want to

*th*ee one *th*cratch on that machine!"

Agent P gave Dr. Doofenshmirtz a thumbs-up. He had every intention of returning Norm as quickly as possible—just as soon as his mission was complete!

Back at home, Candace was carefully guarding her laptop and the precious CD that was inside it. She knew she would have to stay up all night to protect it. It was going to be a long night—but *so* worth it.

"Hey, Candace, Ferb wants to get started on the multimedia presentation for Mom," Phineas said. "Can we borrow the CD?"

He reached out to grab it, but Candace shooed him away. "No way, Phineas!" she snapped. She held the shiny CD high in the air. "There's no way I'm letting this out of my sight. This is the single greatest moment of my life! And there is nothing you can do to take it away from me!"

Just then, an enormous face appeared at the window. It was Norm, the giant robot!

"Hello, children!" his robotic voice boomed out as he grabbed the roof over the bedroom and lifted it up! His massive metal hand reached down and plucked the CD from Candace's fingers. "I'll take that," Norm said.

Then he slipped the disk into his wallet and tucked it into his pocket. He carefully replaced the roof and headed down the street, leaving an astonished Candace, Phineas, and Ferb behind.

"What . . . was . . . *that*?" Candace stammered, shocked.

"I don't know, but it was cool!" Phineas replied in amazement.

Candace looked at her brothers curiously. "So . . . you guys didn't make that?"

"No, but I want one!" Phineas exclaimed.

"That thing ran off with my disk!" Candace cried. "My evidence!"

"Don't worry, Candace," Phineas said kindly. "We'll help you get it back.

"You guys would help me bust you?" she asked.

"Sure, if it will make you happy," Phineas replied. "Plus, battling a giant robot—how cool is that?"

"Excellent," Candace said with a smile. She ran outside, with Phineas and Ferb following behind her. They jumped on their bikes and raced down the street.

It wasn't hard to find Norm. The giant robot

was stomping down the street, smashing fire hydrants and crushing fences. "What a lovely evening!" Norm announced.

"There he is!" Candace shouted.

Norm's head rotated around. Inside, Agent P watched a monitor that showed Phineas, Ferb, and Candace quickly approaching. The platypus carefully pushed a series of buttons. It was his job as Agent P to make sure that the kids didn't get hold of the disk!

"Uh-oh. We need to get the lead out!" Norm declared cheerfully. "Switching to hypertransportation mode!"

Suddenly, wheels and rockets sprung out of the robot's shoes. In an instant, Norm

zoomed down the street, leaving a trail of smoke behind him.

Phineas, Ferb, and Candace watched in awe. Did they really just see that?

"We're going to need a faster bike!" Phineas declared.

Meanwhile, Major Monogram waited impatiently in a high-tech conference room. He glanced around the table at all the secret agents he had assembled—but one chair was empty. It was impossible not to notice that his best agent was missing.

"Any word from Agent P?" Major Monogram asked his intern Carl Karl, who stood dutifully by his side.

"No, sir," Carl replied.

Major Monogram nodded. "So, I guess all we can do is wait," he said.

"And hope, sir," Carl added.

"And hope," agreed Major Monogram. He sighed and looked at his team of secret agents. He decided that everyone in the conference room would benefit from a change in mood. "So, anyone know any good songs?" he asked. "How about you, Agent D?"

Agent D, a dog wearing a fedora, barked in response.

Major Monogram turned to another agent. "Agent C?" he asked hopefully.

Agent C, a plump chicken, clucked and started pecking at the table.

Major Monogram shook his head. It was hopeless! "Carl, remind me again why all the agents are animals."

Carl just shrugged in response. He didn't make the rules!

Chapter 4

While Major Monogram tried to lead his secret agents in a sing-along, Agent P skillfully piloted Norm down the dark city streets. He checked the control panel, which was filled with blinking lights and high-tech screens.

As Agent P confirmed the route on an interactive map, a female voice started to talk. "Estimated time to destination: three-point-zero-five minutes," she announced.

“We’ll be there in no time!” Norm’s robotic voice boomed out happily.

Agent P started to relax. There was no sign of Phineas, Ferb, or Candace—the rocket boosters had left them far behind. In just a few minutes, he would personally deliver the CD to Major Monogram. And the risk of discovery would be over!

Suddenly, a loud alarm sounded through the control room. “Warning! Oil level low!” the female voice reported. A flashing graph popped up on the screen. Norm’s water and gas levels were fine, but the giant robot was almost out of oil—and without oil, he would come to a grinding halt!

Agent P looked worried. The last thing he wanted to do was stop for any reason. But if he didn't, the whole mission would be in jeopardy. So, reluctantly, he steered Norm into an all-night gas station.

"I could sure use an oily beverage!" Norm called out.

Agent P parked the robot in front of the pumps. He pressed the controls to lift up Norm's head so that he could pop out of the control room and help Norm refuel. There wasn't a moment to lose!

Agent P quickly ran over to the attendant and bought every can of oil in stock. He wasn't sure how much oil a giant robot needed to run at rocket speed, but Agent P wasn't going to take any chances!

* * *

Back at agency headquarters, Major Monogram hadn't given up on leading a secret-agent sing-along. He took out his guitar and decided to lead the agents in a new song that he'd written himself.

Strumming a few chords repeatedly, Major Monogram sang, "And the kitty goes—"

That was Agent K's cue. *"Meow!"*

"And the owl goes—" continued Major Monogram.

"Hoo! Hoo!" Agent O hooted.

"And the doggie goes—" Major Monogram added.

"Woof! Woof!" barked Agent D.

"And that's how the animals go, go, go!" Major Monogram sang. "And that's how the animals go! Okay, everyone, one more time, with feeling!"

But despite his hearty singing, Major Monogram was worried. What could possibly be taking Agent P so long to return with the CD? He could only hope that his best agent hadn't been caught!

High above the city, Agent P poured can after can of oil into Norm's tank. Suddenly, the platypus heard a strange noise. He grabbed his binoculars to get a closer look.

There, on the street below, a bicycle was zooming toward the giant robot. But not just any bike. This bike had an enormous rocket strapped to it, and it was carrying Phineas, Ferb, and Candace!

"Good thing we had this extra rocket engine, huh?" Phineas yelled. He and Ferb were loving every minute of the crazy ride!

Candace, however, was terrified. She couldn't even speak.

Agent P knew he didn't have a moment to lose. He tossed the oil cans overboard and leaped back into the control room in Norm's head. With a deafening roar, Agent P fired up Norm's rockets and the robot zoomed off down the street.

"Whoa!" Norm yelled. "Here we go again!"

But there was a problem—a *big* problem. Slippery, shiny black oil spurted out of Norm's tank, coating the robot and the street below. Norm's head began to turn around in a complete circle!

"Uh-oh! Someone forgot to replace the oil cap!" Norm announced cheerfully.

The enormous robot started to malfunction immediately. The wheels on his shoes popped off, and the rocket blasters soon followed.

"I guess I'm walking!" Norm reported as he started to lumber down the street, the pavement shaking with every step he took.

Without the rockets and wheels, it was impossible for Norm to outrun Phineas, Ferb, and Candace on their rocket-powered bike. And to make matters worse, the drawbridge ahead was about to open!

But Agent P knew he had no choice. He had to get Norm over the drawbridge if he wanted to safely deliver the CD to his headquarters. Major Monogram—and the entire society of secret agents—was counting on him!

So, fully aware of the risks, Agent P pushed Norm to cross the drawbridge as it started to open. With a little luck, Norm would make it over the bridge just in time—stranding

Phineas, Ferb, and Candace on the other side!

But luck was not on Agent P's side tonight. The bridge opened wider and wider—and Norm found himself stuck with one foot on each side of it!

Just then, Phineas, Ferb, and Candace arrived. Candace was hysterical and screaming at the top of her lungs. As the rocket-bike screeched to a halt, Ferb was propelled into the air. He landed just a few feet away from the robot and ran as fast as he could to tackle it.

"Go get him, Ferb!" Phineas cheered.

Ferb took a flying leap and landed on Norm's back. He wrapped his arms around the front of the robot—and was ready to take back the disk!

But Norm was still covered in slippery oil. Before Ferb could grab the CD, he started to slip down the robot. As he slid, he came closer and closer to falling into the river below!

Inside the robot, Agent P frantically pushed some controls to make Norm twist around. He hoped that the motions would make Ferb fly off Norm and land safely on the other side of the bridge—instead of landing in the water.

And that's exactly what happened! Covered in slippery oil, Ferb slid down the bridge to the street below.

But Agent P's concern for Ferb had made things much worse for Norm. As the bridge continued to open, Norm stretched from tiptoe to tiptoe to cover the gap. Suddenly, he flipped over, hanging upside down from the bridge.

"Boy, I'm sure in a pickle," Norm reported

as the oil made it even harder for him to balance on the edges of the bridge.

Phineas saw his chance to rescue the CD. He raced up the bridge, across Norm's legs, and plucked it from the robot's pocket!

"Whoo-hoo!" Candace yelled.

But the slippery oil and smooth metal made Norm slide down the bridge even faster. "Perhaps I should have worn cleats," he commented.

Agent P knew he was in trouble—*big* trouble. Not only had he lost the CD again, but now Norm was about to fall into the river! And to make matters worse, Norm wasn't the only one heading for disaster. Phineas was still standing on the upside-down robot, and now he was covered in oil, too!

As Norm slipped even closer to falling completely off the bridge, Phineas took a big risk: he made a daring leap and grabbed the edge of the bridge just before Norm plunged into the river!

The disk flew out of Phineas's hand and wobbled on the edge of the bridge. Phineas tried with all his might to hold on—but his hands were covered in slick oil that made it impossible to get a good grip. He was slipping off the bridge, just like Norm had!

"Candace, help!" Phineas yelled. "The oil! I'm slipping!"

Candace raced to the edge of the bridge, "I'm coming!" she shouted. "Hold on, Phineas!"

But when she reached the edge, Candace realized that she had to make a difficult choice.

Both Phineas and the disk were about to fall into the river—and she could only save one of them! How would she ever make such a tough decision?

"Candace!" Phineas cried as he started to lose his grip.

Candace knew what she had to do. She leaped forward and grabbed Phineas's hands, just as he was about to fall into the water below!

But by rescuing Phineas, she had lost the CD. It teetered back and forth once more before falling off the side of the bridge.

"But Candace!" Phineas gasped. "The disk! You didn't save it!"

"What? And let you fall?" asked Candace. "You may be a pain, but you *are* my brother." Candace reached down to give Phineas a big hug. Then she flashed him a smile. "Besides, I still have that big rocket for evidence!" She turned around to point at the rocket-bike that Phineas and Ferb had built.

But there, lying on the bridge, was only the bike. The rocket had disappeared!

"What happened to the rocket?" Candace asked, confused.

Suddenly, Phineas and Candace heard a loud noise. They looked up to see the rocket flying in a loop before it exploded in a million dazzling, hot pink sparks! The rocket was

gone—and so was Candace's evidence.

"Hmm," Phineas said thoughtfully. "Good thing we got off of that, huh?"

Just then, Ferb, wearing a backpack with a helicopter propeller attached to it, flew up from the river. Phineas and Candace looked at him in amazement. But even more amazing was the fact that Ferb had somehow grabbed the CD!

"All right, Ferb! Cool!" Phineas and Candace cheered.

But Ferb didn't pilot his helicopter backpack into landing next to his siblings. Instead, he flew right over them!

"Ferb? *Ferb?* Where are you going?" called Candace.

"Ferb?" Phineas yelled.

But Ferb just flew farther away, never even looking back.

As the drawbridge closed, something even stranger happened: Ferb slid down to Candace and Phineas, covered in slick, black oil.

"What did I miss?" Ferb asked.

"Huh?" said Candace, who was utterly confused. Wasn't Ferb just flying in the sky a second ago?

"Well, that was almost weirder than the giant robot," Phineas remarked. He looked over at Candace. If this was the real Ferb, then who was piloting the helicopter backpack?

Chapter 5

As soon as he was out of sight of Candace, Phineas, and Ferb, Agent P unzipped his Ferb disguise and tossed it aside. It was so much easier to pilot the helicopter backpack without wearing that costume!

Agent P flew back to his agency's headquarters as quickly as possible. When he arrived, all the

secret agents, Carl, and Major Monogram were still waiting for him in the conference room.

"Agent P!" Major Monogram exclaimed, sounding extremely relieved. "I trust that your mission was a complete success?"

The platypus nodded. He proudly walked up to the table and presented the CD to his superior officer.

"Good work," Major Monogram replied. "Now hand it over for the special disposal procedure."

After Major Monogram put on a pair of protective rubber gloves, Agent P slid the CD across the table. Major Monogram picked it up as carefully as he could. Then Carl approached carrying a special pair of sturdy tongs.

“Careful!” warned Major Monogram as Carl used the tongs to gently lift the disk. Then Carl marched over to an ordinary trash can—and dropped the disk inside. “Got it!” he exclaimed.

If he wasn’t such a professional, Agent P would have rolled his eyes. All that work, all those special precautions—just to throw the disk away in a regular garbage can!

But Agent P knew better than to question Major Monogram’s instructions. After all, they always managed to prevent evil somehow.

"Agent P, you've saved this organization," Major Monogram said gratefully. "If there's anything we can do for you in return, don't hesitate to ask."

Agent P raised his eyebrows. There *was* one thing he could think of. . . .

The next day, Mr. Fletcher got another surprise in the mail. "Oh, I can't believe it!" he exclaimed.

Phineas, Ferb, and Candace stopped what they were doing and looked at their dad.

"It seems my video traffic ticket's been cleared!" their father continued happily. He pointed up toward the ceiling. "I guess there really *is* someone up there looking out for me!"

Mr. Fletcher was absolutely right—because

at the top of the stairs, watching his family below, sat Perry the Platypus!

Back at agency headquarters, Major Monogram and the other secret agents decided to kick back and relax a little. Now that the danger of being revealed as secret agents had passed, the crew was ready to have a little fun! And what better way to have fun than with another sing-along!

So once again, Major Monogram brought out his guitar. He sat on the floor and strummed his favorite chords as Agent C,

Agent D, and Agent W the worm crowded around him.

"Oh, the chicken goes—" sang Major Monogram.

"*Cluck!*" replied Agent C.

"And the dog goes—" Major Monogram continued.

"*Woof!*" barked Agent D.

"And the worm goes—" Major Monogram belted out.

There was silence as Agent W had his very first solo.

"Outstanding, Agent W!" cheered Major Monogram.

Agent C thought Agent W did a fine job, too—and that he also looked like a fine snack! The chicken couldn't help itself and started pecking at the ground around Agent W.

"Agent C!" Major Monogram shouted. "Don't do that." Then he picked up his guitar and started strumming again to get the song

back on track. "And the new guy goes—" he sang.

"I'm Norm!" a giant metal robot announced suddenly. Somehow the robot had made it out of the river and found the secret spy headquarters!

Major Monogram frowned and stopped playing. "You know, Carl, it's weird that he's not an animal," he said. "We should fire him."

Carl whipped a clipboard out of his back pocket and made note. "I'm already on it, sir!"

Major Monogram breathed a sigh of relief.

The disk was secure; Agent P's identity was still secret; and by the end of the day, all the agents would be animals. Everything was just the way it should be.

No wonder Major Monogram felt like singing!

Part Two

Chapter 1

The beautiful summer day was suddenly pierced by an earsplitting shriek. "Oh, my gosh, Stacy! Oh, my gosh! Jeremy asked me if I could meet him at the fair later today next to the Ferris wheel!" Candace Flynn squealed into her cell phone. She was chatting with her best friend, Stacy Hirano.

Candace beamed. She had a huge crush on Jeremy Johnson, and now he wanted to hang

out with her at the fair. And maybe even ride the Ferris wheel together!

Suddenly, Candace's smile disappeared. "Oh, no," she groaned. "I almost forgot: I'm scared of heights! What am I going to do?"

Just then, her mother called out, "Candace! We're leaving now!"

"Mom!" Candace yelled back. "I'm having a teenage crisis!"

"Don't forget, we'll be going bowling," Mrs. Flynn replied calmly. "We need you to keep an eye on the boys."

"Preferably *two* eyes!" joked Mr. Fletcher, Candace's dad.

The boys in question—Candace's younger brothers, Phineas Flynn and Ferb Fletcher—stood next to their parents and grinned at each other. "Bowling? That sounds fun!" Phineas exclaimed. "Hey, Dad, is it all right if we use that old lawn-bowling set?"

"Sure thing, boys," his father replied. "Knock yourselves out."

"Toodles!" Mrs. Flynn called. She and her husband picked up their striped bowling bags and headed out the door.

Candace flopped back on her bed, clutching her phone to her ear. Her personal Ferris-wheel crisis was *far* too important to be interrupted by her brothers!

Downstairs, Phineas and Ferb were very excited. They grabbed the lawn-bowling kit and carried it outside.

"You know, Ferb, with a few modifications, we could really zip up this old lawn-bowling set," Phineas said as he examined the well-worn pins.

"Hello, Phineas!" a voice suddenly called out.

It was Phineas and Ferb's friend Baljeet Patel. "What are you doing?" he asked.

"We're going to build the world's biggest and best bowling-ball game!" Phineas declared. Ferb nodded enthusiastically.

Baljeet grinned and held up a thick book. "Well, according to *The Most Pointless Book of World Records*—"

All of a sudden, Baljeet was interrupted by a blaring noise. The neighborhood bully, Buford Van Stomm, had arrived and was playing the trumpet.

Baljeet paused until the music ended, and then he continued talking. "The world's largest bowling ball is four feet in diameter," he reported.

Phineas's eyes widened. "*Four* feet?" he repeated. "Ferb, we can beat that record in our sleep!"

"You know, the officials from *The Most Pointless Book of World Records*—" Baljeet began. But once again, he had to stop talking because of Buford's trumpet playing.

As soon as the music stopped, Bajeet continued. "Will be at the fair today at three o'clock, handing out awards," Baljeet finally finished.

"Ferb, get the tools," Phineas said quickly. "We've got a record to shatter!"

Baljeet raised his book high in the air. "And then you will be in the next volume of—"

Yet again, he was interrupted by Buford. With a frown, Baljeet turned around.

"Is that absolutely necessary?" Baljeet asked him.

"Why? Does it bug you?" Buford replied.

"Well, yes—a little," Baljeet admitted.

"Then, yeah, it's necessary," Buford said with a smirk.

"All right," Baljeet sighed. "Fair enough." Then Baljeet looked around the backyard. "Hey," he said. "Where's Perry?"

Phineas and Ferb shrugged. It wasn't at all unusual for their pet platypus, Perry, to disappear for hours at a time. They always figured that he was sleeping in some dark, cozy place, like under the bed.

But they couldn't have been more wrong! In reality, Perry the Platypus was actually a secret agent, whose code name was Agent P. It was Agent P's mission in life to track down the evil Dr. Doofenshmirtz and put a stop to his terrible plots.

At Perry's agency headquarters, Major Monogram and his dedicated assistant, Carl Karl, collected data about Dr. Doofenshmirtz's latest evil schemes. And whenever Major Monogram had enough information about a particular plot, he summoned Agent P to put an immediate stop to it.

At that very moment, Agent P was about to escape through a hollow opening in a tree to get to his headquarters. As he zoomed through a series of underground pipes, he suddenly fell out of one of them and landed in a cold, wet puddle on the ground!

"Oh, sorry about that, Agent P!" Carl exclaimed as he dropped his wrench. He had removed a leaky section of one of the underground pipes to repair it—which put a serious kink in Agent P's quick approach to his headquarters!

In one fast motion, Carl picked up Agent P and tossed him back in the pipe. *Whoosh!* The platypus zoomed off once again.

When Agent P finally arrived, Major Monogram was waiting for him. The platypus climbed into a bright orange captain's chair, right in front of the enormous flat-screen video monitor that broadcasted an image of his superior officer.

"Good morning, Agent P," Major Monogram said. "We've tracked Dr. Doofenshmirtz to an old abandoned warehouse, and he's made some suspicious purchases: ten thousand packets of powdered hot chocolate, a hot dog vendor's cart, a medium-size parka, and

a pair of red flannel long johns."

Agent P raised his eyebrows. That list of items sounded *extremely* suspicious—especially since it involved Dr. Doofenshmirtz.

"Don't ask us how we know," continued Major Monogram. "Get out there and kick some Doofen-butt!"

Agent P didn't need to hear another word. He blasted his grappler gun and held on tight. The iron claw and steel cable would zip him out of the headquarters in no time.

And it was probably safer than trying to travel through the pipes again—at least until Carl had finished the repairs!

Chapter 2

Back at home, Phineas and Ferb were building a steel frame in the shape of a sphere for their enormous bowling ball. They covered it with curved metal panels. Then the fun really started as they developed a high-tech control panel to be placed inside the ball. Finally, they installed a pilot's chair with the very latest in safety devices and a flat-screen monitor so that anyone piloting the bowling

ball could see what was happening outside of it.

After all, what was the point of building the world's biggest bowling ball if you couldn't ride around in it?

Baljeet was amazed at the giant ball sitting in Phineas and Ferb's backyard. He was so impressed that he hardly noticed Phineas and Ferb leaning against it, fast asleep.

"Wow! That is one big bowling ball!" Baljeet exclaimed.

Baljeet's voice woke the stepbrothers. "Hey, look at that, Ferb," Phineas said. "Told you we could do it in our sleep."

Upstairs in her bedroom, Candace was back on the phone, chatting with Stacy. "So, what do you think I should wear to the fair tonight?" Candace asked. "I'm thinking my favorite red

blouse with my white skirt and matching red socks."

Suddenly, Candace was interrupted by a tremendously loud noise that shook the entire house. Her eyes narrowed. There was only one explanation for that kind of sound.

Phineas and Ferb were up to something!

"Stacy, I'm going to have to call you back," Candace told her friend. Then she raced down the stairs.

Outside, the huge bowling ball was rolling straight toward a giant set of pins!

Crash!

As the ball smashed into the pins, every one of them toppled over! A crowd of kids that had gathered in the backyard clapped and cheered.

"That was amazing!" Phineas exclaimed as he climbed out of the bowling ball. He smiled at his friends.

"Wow, Phineas!" cried his friend Isabella Garcia-Shapiro. "Another strike!"

"That makes four in a row," Phineas said proudly. "In your face, Buford!"

"Ha, ha!" Baljeet laughed. "Yes! What he said! Ha, ha, ha!"

But when Buford stood over Baljeet and gave him a mean stare, the laughter stopped.

"Uh . . . I mean, you will get him next time, clearly," Baljeet said nervously.

"Ferb, did you get that strike?" Phineas asked.

Ferb, who was wearing a sun visor and a bowling shirt, nodded. He knew that keeping score was not a job to be taken lightly. He pressed a button and a machine put the pins back in formation.

"Who's next?" Phineas asked his friends as he glanced around the yard. But before anyone could volunteer, Candace marched up to them.

"Phineas, just *what* do you think you're doing out here?" she yelled.

"Candace, you're just in time," replied Phineas. "It's your turn!"

Candace glared at Phineas and grabbed her cell phone. "Just *wait* until Mom hears about . . ." she began.

Then Candace paused. An idea had just occurred to her. "But then again, you guys *always* seem to make everything disappear before Mom gets home. But if I take the evidence to her at the Bowl-R-Ama, then she'll *have* to believe me!"

Candace could see it now: her mom rushing over to her, saying, "Oh, *Candace*! You were right about Phineas and Ferb this whole time! We should have believed you!"

Her dad would chime in, waving a credit card in the air. "And to express how sorry we are, here's my credit card. You have our permission to ruin us financially!"

Just when it seemed Candace's daydream couldn't get any better, Jeremy appeared in it! And he was holding a velvet jewelry box! "Candace, that is so cool how you busted your brothers," he said. "Will you marry me?"

"So, you want to give it a try?" Phineas asked Candace.

"I do, Jeremy," Candace said happily as she stared into space. Then she shook herself out of her daydream. There was only one way to make her fantasy a reality: take the giant bowling ball to the Bowl-R-Ama to prove to

her parents that what she said about her brothers was true! "I mean, uh . . . I'd love to give it a try," she told her brother.

"All right!" Phineas cheered. He opened the door to the bowling ball, and he and Candace climbed inside. "I'll show you how it works. Well, first of all, the cockpit's on a gyroscope so it stays level. Here's your monitor, and this is the trackball you use to steer," he explained. "Now, no matter what, never hit the gyrostabilizer lock button. It'll disable the gyroscope, and you'll spin around."

"Yeah, yeah," Candace said impatiently. "Use the trackball, don't hit the button. I got it."

"All right, you seem to know what you're doing," Phineas replied as he climbed out of the bowling ball.

"Do I *ever!*" Candace cackled gleefully. She

buckled her safety belt. "This is a piece of cake. Bowl-R-Ama, here I come!"

"Okay, Candace, try to take it slow at first," Phineas warned her from outside.

But Candace had no intention of taking it slow. She giggled hysterically as she started to wildly spin the trackball. All of a sudden, the bowling ball shot off, knocking down all the pins at top speed!

"Way to go, Candace!" yelled Phineas.

But the bowling ball didn't stop there. It zoomed through the yard, smashing into the scoring table. Then it crushed the fence and rolled right into the street!

"Where's she going?" Phineas gasped.

All the kids raced into the front yard and stared after the speeding bowling ball. Suddenly, Phineas grinned. "She's free-styling!" he exclaimed. "We've got to follow her and see what she does. Let's go, team!"

Phineas, Ferb, Isabella, Baljeet, and Buford

split up and raced back to their own houses. Each one collected his or her own means of transportation: Phineas hopped on his red scooter; Ferb jumped on his yellow-and-black mountain bike; Isabella laced up her white-and-pink roller skates; Baljeet climbed on his unicycle; and Buford grabbed his skateboard.

In moments, they met up again in front of Phineas and Ferb's house. Then they raced after the bowling ball.

Wherever Candace was going, they were ready to follow!

Chapter 3

Across town, Agent P held on tightly to a long cable as he swung through a window into a run-down, old building. But this wasn't just any building—it was Doofenshmirtz Abandoned Self-Storage, where the evil doctor's latest plot was being planned!

Agent P landed on the floor and glanced around. The room was covered in frost and icicles. It was bitterly cold inside. But before

the platypus could figure out what was going on, an enormous mechanical penguin waddled up to him—and blasted him with an ice ray. Now Perry was trapped in a block of ice!

There was no doubt in Agent P's mind that Dr. Doofenshmirtz was behind the ice-blasting penguin, so he wasn't a bit surprised when the evil doctor appeared in a purple parka with a fur-trimmed hood.

"Ah, Perry the Platypus, right on time!" Dr. Doofenshmirtz laughed from an elevated platform. "It seems like you got *quite* a chill there!"

Agent P wished he could have rolled his eyes at Dr. Doofenshmirtz's lame joke. But he couldn't move a muscle.

"I want you to meet my latest creation,"

the doctor continued. "The Giant-Robotic-Penguin-Icy-Freeze-Your-Socks-Off-Breath-inator . . . thingy. First, I will unleash my giant penguins at the fair today so they may begin freezing the entire city. Then, I will sell all the citizens of Danville my organic, yet highly addictive Doof Brand hot chocolate."

Dr. Doofenshmirtz paused as he imagined the ice-covered streets of Danville crowded with shivering people. And in the middle of them all, a hot-chocolate cart next to a giant steaming mug filled with his supersecret hot chocolate!

"Because, you know, who doesn't enjoy a nice cup of hot chocolate when it's so cold out?" Dr. Doofenshmirtz asked. "The first cup will be free, of course. But then the *second* will also be free . . . but then the *third* will cost a million dollars! That way, I only have to sell three and I will already be a millionaire!"

Perry could do nothing but watch helplessly as Dr. Doofenshmirtz's army of robotic penguins paraded through the room and headed outside.

Agent P was so solidly frozen into the block of ice that he couldn't even shiver, let alone chase after the evil doctor. But that wasn't about to stop him from saving the day.

After all, the citizens of Danville—and the entire tri-state area—were counting on him!

Meanwhile, Phineas, Ferb, and their friends continued to follow the bowling ball that

Candace was piloting. Suddenly, Phineas realized where Candace was going. "She's headed for the Bowl-R-Ama!" he exclaimed.

Just then, Mrs. Flynn glanced at her phone. "You know, dear, Candace hasn't called," she said to her husband.

"Oh, don't worry," he replied. "I'm sure the kids are having a ball."

At that very moment, the enormous bowling ball zoomed right past Phineas and Ferb's parents toward the Bowl-R-Ama entrance! But just as it was ready to plow through the building's doors, a van that was about to park

in front of the bowling alley knocked the ball off-course. The ball rolled down a hill, gaining speed every second!

"Ooh, that's gotta hurt," Phineas commented when the car hit the ball.

"Oh, no!" shrieked Candace from inside the bowling ball. She tried to steer the trackball but it popped out of position and bounced around. Now the bowling ball was speeding out of control!

The ball raced past a construction site, then dropped into a pit and rolled through a large pipe. Phineas rode up to a group of construction workers, with his friends right behind him. "So, where does this lead?" he asked the crew.

One of the construction workers grunted. "Heck if I know!"

"Ferb, the map of Danville's underground," Phineas requested.

Ferb handed him a set of rolled-up blueprints. Phineas opened them to reveal a diagram of a series of connected tubes—a map of all the pipes and tunnels that lay hidden beneath the streets of Danville.

"Looks like she's headed downtown!" Phineas announced. Then he took off after the bowling ball, with everyone else following along behind him.

Meanwhile, inside the ball, Candace was panicking. "Stop, stop, stop, stop, stop!" she screamed as the ball tumbled over and over. Suddenly, it shot into a long tunnel and landed on some tracks, slowing down before it came to a complete halt.

"Oh, good," Candace said, sighing. "It stopped."

Then she peeked at the monitor, and a look of horror crossed her face.

The bowling ball had stopped on the *subway* tracks.

And a train was headed her way!

"Wait!" she shrieked. "Go, go, go, go, go!"

But it was too late! The train knocked into the bowling ball and sent it rolling down the tunnel. Then another train knocked it in a different direction. Then yet another train sent the bowling ball zooming along as if it were part of a giant game of pinball! It passed by a platform where two men were waiting for the subway.

"That's one big bowling ball, Bob," one of the men remarked.

"You betcha, Barry," his friend agreed.

Phineas, Ferb, and their friends arrived on the platform just in time to see the bowling ball speed down the tracks.

"Here she comes," Phineas called.

"Go, Candace!" yelled Baljeet and Buford.

"And there she goes," Buford added as the ball zipped away.

"All right, guys. To Seventh Street!" Phineas commanded. "Go, Candace!"

All the kids cheered as they sped off after the bowling ball. This was one wild ride that they didn't want to miss!

Chapter 4

Phineas, Ferb, Baljeet, Isabella, and Buford raced out of the subway station just in time to see the giant bowling ball—with Candace still inside it—blast out of the tunnel and onto the sidewalk.

"Go, Candace!" the kids screamed.

The bowling ball crashed into a courtyard, bouncing back and forth against several newsstands. The metal stands made a *ping-ping-ping* noise whenever the ball hit them.

That gave Phineas a great idea. "Hey, Baljeet!" he called. "What's the world record for the largest pinball machine?"

"I'm not sure," replied Baljeet as he flipped through his book of world records. "But I know we can beat it!"

"Okay, everybody," Phineas said. "Split up, and let's keep the ball in play until we get to the fair!"

With a little bit of luck, Phineas knew

that they could turn the entire city of Danville into one enormous pinball game! The kids rode off, forming an arc to surround the bowling ball so that they could follow it wherever it went. The ball sped down the street as Phineas and Ferb tailed it.

Inside the bowling ball, Candace held on to her chair as tightly as she could. She was very grateful that Phineas and Ferb had installed such strong safety belts! Unfortunately the trackball was useless. As it bounced around inside the bowling ball, it suddenly slammed into the gyrostabilizer button—the *one* button that Phineas had warned Candace not to touch!

A loud alarm blared through the bowling ball. Candace's steady and sturdy chair was no longer locked in place. Now she, too, was being

bounced around inside the bowling ball!

"*Ahhhhhhhhhhh*! I'm out of control!" Candace shrieked as she tumbled over and over.

The speeding bowling ball rolled along a curved wall and bounced off an open door. Then it zipped by a row of turnstiles, hitting each one with a loud noise before it bounced over them and rolled away.

Next, the ball sped past the golden statues of athletes in front of the Danville Arena. *Ping!* It bounced off a golden hockey stick. *Pang!* It knocked against the soccer player statue's golden foot. Then it barreled through a row of parked cars, right toward the Super Food Stuff Mart—and all of the unsuspecting shoppers inside!

Baljeet knew just what to do. He raced ahead of the rolling ball and got into position just beyond the store's automatic doors. When the bowling ball approached, Baljeet leaped in

front of the doors. *Whoosh!* The doors swung open, knocking the bowling ball away from the store!

Phineas sped up on his scooter. He had a feeling the ball was now heading toward the movie theater. Phineas got there right before the bowling ball did. He leaped off his scooter and kicked open the doors—just in time for the ball to zip through them! All the lights on the movie theater's marquee lit up and started flashing. It

looked like Phineas had hit the giant pinball jackpot!

"*Woo-hoo!*" he cheered.

Then the ball sped back out of the theater and rolled away at top speed, right toward the city bridge. If it crossed the bridge out of Danville, it would be in another town—and a lot harder for the kids to control! Uh-oh. What were they going to do now?

Chapter 5

Luckily, Ferb was on top of the problem. He raced into the bridge's control tower. Before the bridge operator could react, Ferb pressed a button that opened the bridge so that tall boats could sail through. The bridge popped open—knocking the bowling ball back into Danville!

As the bowling ball continued to pick up speed, everyone had to work even harder to keep it from causing a catastrophe of enormous proportions! But they were up to the challenge. Isabella moved an elderly lady safely out of the way as the ball zipped into a shopping mall. The ball raced up and down escalators and along the sleek walkways of the mall as shoppers watched in amazement. It bounced off fountains and vendor carts and information booths.

"Ahhhhhhhhhh!" Candace kept screaming, getting dizzier by the second.

The bowling ball traveled even faster as it rolled out of the shopping mall, right toward a dump truck filled with wet cement. But the cement didn't slow the ball down at all. Instead, the truck acted like a ramp: the ball raced up it and flew through the air, crashing into a fruit cart! A wave of fruit pulp splashed onto everyone standing within ten feet.

Ferb calmly walked over to the cart and

kicked away a piece of wood that was propping it up. The bowling ball rolled off the cart and down the street.

"Way to keep it going, Ferb!" Phineas yelled.

The brothers watched the bowling ball as it rolled away. It was heading in the direction of the fair!

At the entrance gates of the fair, a vendor had set up a game called Knock 'Em Down. Each contestant tried to knock down a pyramid of milk bottles by throwing a ball at them. If the contestant won, he or she got to choose a fuzzy stuffed animal hanging from the top of the tent. But what the contestants *didn't* know was that the milk bottles were extraheavy . . . and the ball was extralight. The game was almost impossible to win!

"Oh, better luck next time, little man!" the vendor, who was named Shady Joe, called out to a disappointed little boy who had failed to knock down even one milk bottle. Shady Joe tried his best to look sympathetic. Then his face brightened when Isabella skated up to the game.

"Isabella, darlin'!" Shady Joe exclaimed.

"Set me up, Shady Joe," Isabella said as she slapped a dollar on the counter. She gave him a big smile. "I'm feeling lucky!"

"Oh, that's my girl!" Shady Joe exclaimed as he handed Isabella one of the balls. "You give it your best shot!"

Shady Joe stepped aside so that Isabella would have plenty of room to wind up and throw the ball. While his back was turned, Isabella stepped aside, too.

Crash! Suddenly the giant bowling ball smashed through the booth, knocking down every single milk bottle—and all the stuffed animals, too!

Shady Joe frowned. So someone had *finally* beaten his fixed game. "Help yourself," he said sadly to Isabella as he gestured to the pile of scattered stuffed animals. "Anything from the top shelf."

At that moment, a voice boomed over the loudspeaker.

"Welcome, Danvillians, to the 'World's Most Pointless World Records Awards!'" the announcer said. A few people from the fair gathered around a stage with a red velvet curtain. They wanted a chance to see who—or what—had broken the records!

"Let's meet some of our record holders!" the announcer continued. "Here we have Cletus, with the 'World's Hairiest Pig.'"

A farmer stepped forward carrying a very large, very hairy pig. He waved to the audience.

"Next to him is Margaret, with the 'World's Stinkiest Cheese,'" the announcer yelled.

Margaret stepped forward and held a wedge of cheese up to the crowd. But she wasn't taking any chances. The stinky cheese was enclosed in a special protective case, and Margaret was wearing a space suit to protect her from the cheese's overpowering smell!

"And finally, we have Little Timmy, holding the 'World's Fattest Gerbil!'" the announcer shouted.

A little boy stepped forward, using both hands to hold up a gerbil cage. The cage was big, but so was the gerbil! It barely fit inside!

"Let's have a big round of applause for the 'World's Most Pointless World Records' winners!" the announcer finished.

As people started to clap politely, Phineas and Ferb raced up to the stage.

"Wait!" Phineas called. "We've got two more 'World's Most Pointless World Records' of our own!"

The announcer grinned at the boys. "Well, then, step right up, and tell everybody what they are!"

Phineas and Ferb climbed onto the stage. The announcer held the microphone out to Phineas.

"Our first entry is for the 'World's Largest Bowling Ball,'" Phineas said into the microphone. "And the other is for the 'World's Longest Game of Pinball!'"

"Wow," the announcer commented. "Well, let's see them!"

Ferb held up his hand. "Wait for it . . ." he said.

Suddenly, Phineas and Ferb's giant bowling ball rolled right past the stage. It bounced around between several game stands, slamming into each one with a loud ring. The

crowd went wild! Everyone was clapping and cheering as the bowling ball turned the entire fair into a huge pinball game!

"Looks like we have two more 'World's Most Pointless Records'!" the announcer exclaimed. Then he gasped. "Wait! *Two* records in *one* day? That's *another* world record!"

Phineas and Ferb grinned at each other. They had hoped they would have an exciting day, but they had never expected to have this much fun!

Chapter 6

Back at Doofenshmirtz Abandoned Self-Storage, Agent P was all alone—and still trapped in a block of solid ice. If he didn't find a way to free himself from his frosty prison, Dr. Doofenshmirtz and his army of ice-breathing robotic penguins would freeze the entire town!

But Agent P had gotten out of seemingly impossible situations before. And he was about to try to do it again!

Several feet away, Dr. Doofenshmirtz had left a steaming mug of Doof Brand hot chocolate on a table. Agent P's eyes narrowed as he stared at the mug. If only there were a way to reach it . . . the heat from the hot chocolate would melt the block of ice, freeing Agent P to foil Dr. Doofenshmirtz's latest evil plot.

With every ounce of his strength, Perry tried to wiggle his toes. At first, nothing happened. And then, suddenly, one of his toes moved! Agent P wiggled his toes back and forth more, which made the block of ice wobble, shaking the ground ever so slightly and making vibrations that reached all the way to the table. Slowly, *slowly*, the cup of hot chocolate moved closer to the edge!

Agent P kept rocking back and forth, never taking his eyes off of the mug. Suddenly, the mug teetered on the edge of the table. Then it fell to the ground and shattered. A steamy river of hot chocolate spilled across the floor—right toward Agent P!

As soon as the hot chocolate hit the ice block, the ice started to crack. Then, with a crash, the block shattered into hundreds of pieces. At last, Agent P was free!

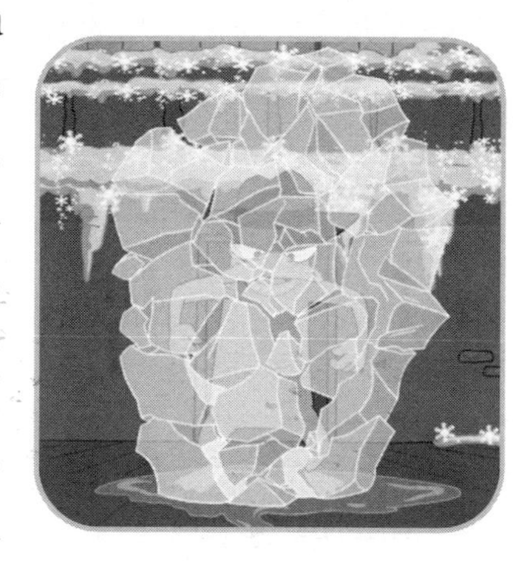

He didn't have a moment to lose. He aimed his grappler gun at the window and blasted it. He held on to the long cord as he catapulted out of the building in the direction of the fair. He had to stop Dr. Doofenshmirtz before it was too late!

Chapter 7

While everyone at the fair cheered for Phineas and Ferb and the world records they'd broken, a mysterious noise boomed throughout Danville, shaking the city streets.

Thud! Thud! Thud! Thud!

The loud noise was coming from Dr. Doofenshmirtz and his army of gigantic robotic penguins! They were approaching the fair—and soon the evil doctor would be able to put his plan into effect, freezing the entire city of Danville!

"To the fair, my pets, where the freezing of the tri-state area will begin!" Dr. Doofenshmirtz cackled as he pushed a cart filled with his homemade hot chocolate.

But just then, Agent P swung up behind the band of robotic penguins. He knew that he had one chance—and one chance only—to act. He fired his grappler gun at a large, curved pipe on top of one of the buildings. When the hook was securely attached to the pipe, Agent P yanked the pipe down. Then he carefully positioned it so that one end faced the group of penguins.

At that very moment, the enormous bowling ball rolled out of the fair. It was

heading straight toward the penguins!

A look of terror crossed Dr. Doofenshmirtz's face. "Wait! Wait, what is that?" he shrieked. "A giant bowling ball? *Nooooo!*"

Dr. Doofenshmirtz stood in front of the animals to protect them, but he was no match for the huge ball. *Smash!* It crashed right through the formation of penguins, knocking them down in a perfect strike!

The impact of the crash sent Dr. Doofenshmirtz flying high into the air. And it knocked Candace right out of the bowling ball and toward the Ferris wheel!

"Ahhhhhhhhhh!" Candace screamed as she flew through the air. She almost sailed over the Ferris wheel but, instead, she landed right next to Jeremy in one of the seats!

"Oh, Candace! You made it!" Jeremy exclaimed. "I was thinking you weren't going to show."

Candace was so shocked to be sitting next

to her crush that she couldn't say a word. And she had completely forgotten that she was afraid of heights! Suddenly, she heard a voice over the loudspeaker.

"We'd especially like to thank our sister, Candace!" Phineas announced from the stage, holding the microphone. Ferb stood next to him, trying to hold their three golden trophies without dropping any. "We couldn't have done it without you, Sis!"

Candace's smile began to fade. She couldn't believe it. Yet again, her brothers had gotten away with everything! And this time, they'd even been awarded *trophies* for their troublemaking!

"You know, your brothers are all right,"

Jeremy said. He pointed to the stage where Phineas and Ferb were waving to the crowd.

Then Jeremy noticed that Candace looked upset. "Hey, are you okay?" he asked.

Candace was speechless. She just pointed at the ground, where Phineas and Ferb basked in the glory of breaking three records in one day.

"Oh, afraid of heights?" Jeremy said sympathetically. He reached his arm around Candace's shoulders. "Don't worry—I've got you!"

As Candace gazed dreamily at Jeremy, her annoyance at Phineas and Ferb melted away.

Far below the Ferris wheel, Phineas noticed that Perry the Platypus had wandered onto the stage. "How about you, Perry?" Phineas asked as he held the microphone out to his pet. "Is there anything you'd like to add?"

Perry just stared blankly ahead and made a noise into the microphone. He wasn't about

to reveal anything that could blow his secret-agent cover!

Across the fair, Shady Joe had cheered up. He'd thought it would take days—or even weeks—to rebuild his game booth and get back to work.

But an unexpected new job opportunity had fallen right into his lap: now Shady Joe was the barker for a sideshow starring a truly bizarre creature!

"Step right up, ladies and gentlemen!" Shady Joe shouted. "It's only a dollar to see the Mysterious Penguin Man! Is he a man? Is he a penguin?"

One by one, people stepped forward to hand Shady Joe a dollar. He held back a velvet curtain and ushered them into a dimly lit room. And there,

sitting on a pile of hay, was a truly disturbing creature.

It was Dr. Doofenshmirtz wearing the head of a robotic penguin! Dr. Doofenshmirtz's own eyes and nose were visible through the penguin's large, gaping beak.

He sighed. "I used to have goals. They were evil goals, but they were goals," he muttered to himself.

Dr. Doofenshmirtz may have been drowning in self-pity, but it was only a matter of time before he got back to cooking up evil plots.

And when that happened, Agent P would be ready for him!

As for Phineas and Ferb, they could hardly believe that they'd shattered so many world records in one day—and all thanks to Candace. It was another totally awesome day of summer vacation!

Don't miss the fun in the next
Phineas & Ferb book . . .

It's Ancient History!

Adapted by Ellie O'Ryan
Based on the series created by Dan Povenmire & Jeff "Swampy" Marsh

When Phineas and Ferb get inspired by the Ancient Greek exhibit at the local museum, they challenge Buford to an awesome chariot race! Who will get to the finish line first? Then, Phineas and Ferb go on an archaeological dig, where they discover a caveman!